Disney's
ONCE UPON A TIME
with
Mary-Kate & Ashley

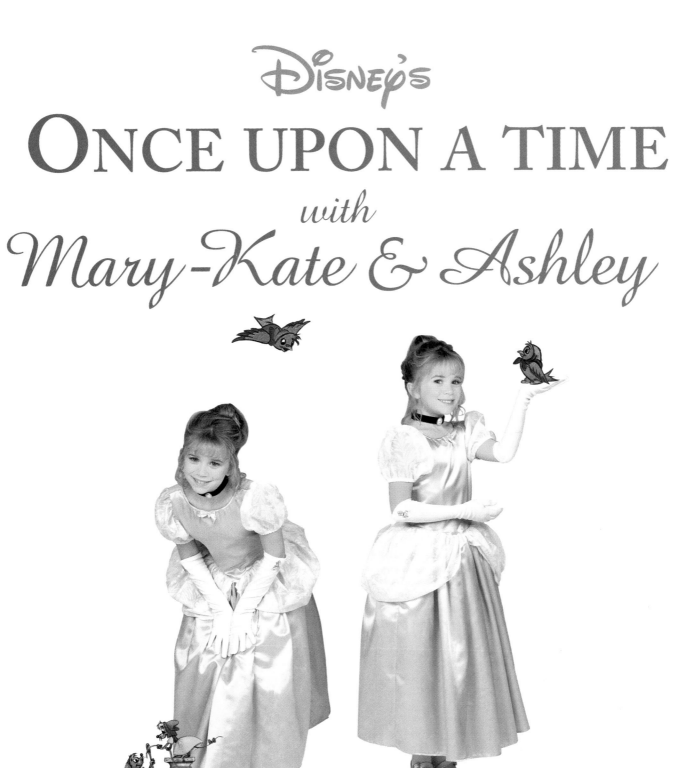

STORIES RETOLD BY GABRIELLE CHARBONNET

DISNEY PRESS

NEW YORK

A PARACHUTE PRESS BOOK

Printed and bound in the United States of America.

Created by Parachute Press, Inc.

First Edition

1 3 5 7 9 10 8 6 4 2

This book is set in 14-point Adobe Caslon.

Library of Congress Cataloging in Publication Card Number 97-80386

ISBN: 0-7868-3189-8

For more Disney Press fun, visit www.DisneyBooks.com

CONTENTS

Hi!

My name is Mary-Kate Olsen.

And my name is Ashley Olsen.

We're the Olsen twins!

We hope you like reading *Once Upon a Time*. These are our six favorite Disney stories ever, because they're about our favorite kind of character: princesses!

There are all different kinds of Disney princess stories, and different kinds of Disney princesses, too. Cinderella is a very kind princess. Snow White is caring and helpful. Ariel is lucky and full of spirit. Belle is really smart, Jasmine is magical, and Pocahontas is the most courageous.

Our favorite stories have lots of action and lots of magic spells. We don't like witches and sorcerers. Too scary! It's a good thing they always lose in the end. That's the best thing about these princess stories: they always have happy endings!

We enjoy the stories even more when we make crafts that remind us of them. Now you can make these special crafts, too! Look for the easy instructions and make a magic wand, a perfect paper rose, even a Dream-Come-True Dream Catcher!

We hope you have lots of fun making our favorite crafts and reading our favorite stories. Or maybe someone will read them to you. We like to take turns reading to each other!

Now it's your turn to curl up with *Once Upon a Time*. We hope you love it as much as we do!

Love,

Mary-Kate & Ashley

Cinderella is my favorite princess story of all. And Cinderella is my favorite princess. She's definitely the most beautiful. And the kindest, too!

That's why it's extra-nice when good things happen to Cinderella. I don't think I could ever be as nice to a family that acted as selfish as Cinderella's stepmother and stepsisters! They make me so mad!

Don't you sometimes wish you had your own fairy godmother? I do. I would wish for some serious things—like making sure no one would ever be mean to me. But I would also wish for fun things—like a pair of glass slippers, just like the ones Cinderella wears to the ball!

It would be fun to get my wishes. But I try to remember that Cinderella's wishes were granted because she was so good and kind. Cinderella really deserves to have her dreams come true. I bet you'll think so, too, after you read her story!

—Mary-Kate

Cinderella

O nce upon a time in a faraway kingdom, there lived a sweet and beautiful little girl. Though she had no mother, she was happy living with her kind father and her many animal friends.

One day this girl's father told her that he planned to marry a woman who had two daughters of her own, Drizella and Anastasia.

"I know you will be glad to have playmates," he said. "And your new stepmother will grow to love you just as much as I do."

But the girl's father died soon after the wedding.

The new stepmother, Lady Tremaine, spoke harshly to her stepdaughter. "You may stay here, but only if you work to earn your keep. Please move your things to a room in the attic."

From that day on, she lived as a servant in her own home. Each day she swept the cinders from the fireplace. Her stepsisters began to call her "Cinderella," and her

life was filled with cooking, cleaning, sewing, and ironing. Yet Cinderella never lost her sweet and kind nature. Somehow, she kept her hopes and dreams alive. She always believed that some day, her life would change.

And until then, she thought, I have my friends to cheer me.

The pretty bluebirds sang to her sweetly, and the scampering mice made her laugh. Two mice, Gus and Jaq, were her special friends.

One morning, as Cinderella scrubbed the floor, there was a loud knocking at the front door. "A message from the king!" a voice announced.

Cinderella flung open the door. A royal messenger handed her a thick envelope. Cinderella felt a burst of excitement. Whatever could the message be?

She hurried upstairs where her stepmother listened to Drizella and Anastasia as they had their music lesson. Cinderella tapped on the door of the music room. Lady Tremaine came to the door with a disapproving frown.

MARY-KATE:
I wonder if we'll be invited to a ball someday.
ASHLEY:
If we are, let's wear matching dresses!

"Excuse me," Cinderella told her. "But this message just arrived from the palace."

"From the palace!" Anastasia gasped.

"Let me see!" Drizella demanded.

"Give it to me," Lady Tremaine ordered. She quickly read the message. "There is to be a grand ball at the palace this very night!" she exclaimed. "The king has ordered every maiden in the kingdom to attend. The young prince is searching for a bride."

"A bride!" Drizella squealed. "He should marry me!"

"No, me!" Anastasia shrieked.

"Stepmother, may I also go to the ball?" Cinderella asked.

Anastasia answered instead. "You? Go to the ball? Wearing one of your patched dresses?"

"And holding your feather duster?" Drizella added. She laughed out loud.

"Now, girls, be fair," Lady Tremaine replied. "The king said every maiden. Of course Cinderella may go to the ball. If she finishes her chores in time."

"Oh, thank you, Stepmother!" Cinderella floated out of the room. A royal ball! It was the most wonderful thing that had ever happened to her. It would be a dream come true!

But I'll need something to wear, Cinderella thought. She flew up the steep, rickety stairs to her small, bare attic room. There, at the bottom of a battered trunk, Cinderella found a gown that had once belonged to her mother. It was very old-fashioned.

Gus, Jaq, and the other mice gathered around as Cinderella studied the dress. "I know I could make this dress as good as new," she said. "Just like this!" She showed her friends a picture of a beautiful ball gown in a book. "I can make it over, if only I have the time."

With a happy smile, Cinderella hurried off. But as the day went on, her stepmother added more and more chores to Cinderella's work. Jaq shook his head. "Poor Cinderella!" he said. "She'll never have a chance to finish her dress."

"She won't be able to go to the ball," Gus added.

"We can help!" a mouse named Blossom exclaimed. "We can fix Cinderella's dress for her. There's nothing to it, really."

"Do you think so?" Jaq asked.

"Yes!" Blossom answered. "You and Gus can gather trimmings from around the castle. The birds will help lift the needle and thread. My friends and I will do the cutting and sewing."

Jaq and Gus quickly searched the house. They found a strand of beads and a pink sash that someone had thrown away. "What a happy surprise for Cinderella!" Jaq cried. He and Gus brought their treasures to the attic room.

It was evening before Cinderella finally finished her work. "I had so many chores," Cinderella murmured. "I never had time to work on my dress!"

Lady Tremaine's carriage pulled up to the front door. Cinderella called to her stepmother and stepsisters. "It is nearly time to leave for the ball," she told them.

"Why, Cinderella," said Lady Tremaine. "You are not ready."

"No," Cinderella replied. "I'm not going to the ball."

Lady Tremaine hid her smile of delight. "That's too bad," she said. "Drizella! Anastasia! Hurry, girls!"

Cinderella dragged herself up to her room. With a sigh, she flung open the door—and was surprised by the bright glow of many candles.

"Why, whatever . . . ," she began. Then she saw it: her mother's old gown looked brand-new!

"Oh, how can I ever thank you?" Cinderella kissed Gus, Jaq, and all her friends. Then she quickly dressed. The gown fit perfectly. Gus and Jaq smiled at how lovely she looked. Cinderella blew them another kiss and hurried down the stairs to the front hall.

"Wait!" she called. "Please! Wait for me!"

Drizella and Anastasia halted in surprise. Lady Tremaine hid her fury. "Girls, don't you like Cinderella's pink sash? And her pretty beads?"

"Those are my beads!" Drizella screeched. She snatched them from Cinderella's neck.

"And that's my sash!" Anastasia shrieked. With one fierce yank, she ripped it from around Cinderella's waist.

"Wait!" Cinderella protested. "Please!"

But the stepsisters pulled and ripped until Cinderella's gown hung in tatters.

"Come, girls," Lady Tremaine called. "We mustn't be late for the ball." She and her daughters climbed into the carriage and were off.

Cinderella ran out to the castle courtyard. She threw herself onto a cold stone bench and sobbed. She felt as if her heart would break.

"It's no use!" she cried. "There's nothing left to believe in."

"If you truly believed in nothing, I wouldn't be here, my dear," a gentle voice replied.

A white-haired woman with a kindly face magically appeared before Cinderella in a glow of fairy lights. "I am your fairy godmother," the woman said. "I'm here to help you."

The fairy godmother pulled a magic wand out of her sleeve.

"First, you'll need a coach!" She pointed the wand at a fat orange pumpkin.

Poof! The pumpkin became a carriage.

Poof! Four mice became a team of white horses.

The fairy godmother gazed at Cinderella. "Goodness, you can't go to the ball dressed like that," she said.

Poof! Cinderella's tattered rags became a beautiful gown.

"Understand that at the stroke of midnight, the spell will be broken," her fairy godmother said as Cinderella climbed into her coach.

"I understand," Cinderella replied. "But it's so much more than I hoped for!"

The team of sparkling white horses carried Cinderella off to the royal palace. The huge ballroom was aglow with a thousand candles. Maidens from all over the kingdom crowded the floor. Yet the Prince hid yawn after yawn. He was bored. Then he spied Cinderella arriving. Her smile was gentle and her eyes were filled with kindness and sweetness. The

Prince hurried to her side.

"May I have this dance?" he asked. He swept Cinderella into his arms.

Cinderella thought the young man was very handsome. They talked and laughed as easily as old friends.

The crowd inside the ballroom buzzed with questions.

"Who is she, Mother?" Anastasia asked.

"Have we seen her before?" Drizella demanded.

"She almost looks familiar," Lady Tremaine replied.

But no one recognized Cinderella. Hours passed, and the palace clock began to strike midnight.

Cinderella gasped. "I must leave!" As she raced down the palace steps, one of her glass

slippers fell off her foot.

Cinderella leaped into her waiting carriage. A short way down the road, the clock struck twelve and the spell was broken. Cinderella was once more dressed in rags. But on one foot she still wore the other glass slipper. "Oh, thank you, Fairy Godmother!" she called.

The next morning, the Grand Duke appeared at the castle door, holding the glass slipper that Cinderella had left at the ball. "By royal command," he announced, "every maiden in the kingdom shall try on this slipper. Whoever it fits shall be the Prince's bride. For he loves the maiden who left it behind."

"The Prince!" Cinderella gasped in surprise.

Lady Tremaine suddenly realized that Cinderella was the unknown girl from the ball.

She locked Cinderella in her room.

"No!" Cinderella cried, beating on the door. "No! You can't do this! Please!"

Lady Tremaine slipped the key into her pocket and went to fetch her daughters. "Get dressed quickly!" she ordered. "One of you may still have a chance to marry the Prince!"

Anastasia was ready first. Lady Tremaine watched hopefully as the grand duke held out the slipper. Anastasia tried to squeeze her large foot into the glass slipper. But she could barely get her big toe inside.

"It's my turn!" Drizella plopped into a chair and held up her foot. It was also too large for the dainty shoe.

"Try harder, you stupid oaf!" Lady Tremaine demanded.

As Drizella tried to squeeze her foot into the slipper, Jaq and Gus sneaked into Lady Tremaine's pocket. They stole the key to Cinderella's room and raced upstairs. They pushed the key under Cinderella's door. Cinderella unlocked it and flew downstairs.

"This slipper fits neither of your daughters." The Duke sighed.

"Wait, please!" Cinderella cried.

Her stepmother and stepsisters stared in horror as Cinderella ran lightly down the stairs.

"Why, she's just the maid!" Anastasia exclaimed.

"Ignore her," Drizella ordered.

The Duke frowned. "My orders are to try the slipper on every maiden," he replied. "Come, my child." The Duke's footman approached Cinderella, holding out the glass shoe. But Lady Tremaine tripped him with her cane. The glass slipper flew through the air and shattered into pieces on the cold marble floor.

"Oh, no!" The Grand Duke moaned in despair.

But Cinderella smiled. "Perhaps this will help," she said, reaching into her pocket. "You see, I have the other slipper."

And so Cinderella and the Prince were married. As they drove off in their wedding carriage, Cinderella knew that dreams really do come true.

MARY-KATE:
Don't you love
happy endings,
Ashley?

ASHLEY:
Totally. Cinderella
is so lucky to have
such good friends—they
really helped make her
dreams come true!

Merry Magic Wand

Mary-Kate and I surprised each other with these magic wands as birthday presents. Why not make magic wands for your friends, too? You'll make them all very merry!

You'll Need

- A small piece of cardboard

- Scissors

- White glue

- A round plastic jewel

- A 24-inch-long wooden dowel, 1/2 inch diameter

- Glitter or sequins

- White ribbon 1/2 inch wide; about three yards

- 2 colored ribbons 1/4 inch wide; about three yards of each

How to Make It

1. Cut out a star shape from the cardboard. Make the star about 4 inches across.

2. Cover one side of the star with glue. Then sprinkle glitter or sequins onto the glued area, making sure the entire surface is covered. Do the same on the other side of the star. When the glue dries, shake off the loose glitter or sequins. Glue a round jewel to the center of one side.

3. Glue the white ribbon to one end of the dowel. Wrap the ribbon around the dowel to the other end. Glue the ribbon to the end.

4. Take one yard of a colored ribbon and glue it to one end of the dowel. Wrap the colored ribbon over the white ribbon. Make sure you can still see the white ribbon underneath. Trim off any extra ribbon at the end and glue the loose end to the stick.

5. Repeat the above steps with one yard of the second colored ribbon.

6. Glue your glitter star to the top of the stick.

7. Cut the remaining 4 yards of colored ribbon into 8 lengths to make ribbon streamers. Glue a cluster of glitter or sequins to the end of each streamer. Tie the plain end of each streamer around the wand, just under the star.

Whenever I think about *Snow White and the Seven Dwarfs*, I picture Snow White running away into the forest. It's so dark and spooky there, and Snow White is all alone! How scary!

The first time I slept outdoors was a little scary. Mary-Kate and I thought it would be fun to sleep in a tent in our backyard. But as soon as we slipped into our sleeping bags, we started imagining spooky things all around us.

Then I remembered that Snow White was afraid at night, too. But in the morning, the forest animals led her to the Seven Dwarfs' cottage. Then she wasn't alone and scared anymore! The next thing I knew, I fell asleep. And in the morning, our dog woke us up and led us inside for breakfast. I felt just like Snow White!

—Ashley

Snow White and the Seven Dwarfs

Once upon a time, there was a young princess who was called Snow White. Her hair was as black as coal and her skin was as white as snow. Snow White was beautiful. But she was also good, truthful, and kind.

Snow White lived in a castle with her stepmother, the Queen. The Queen was also beautiful—on the outside. Inside, she was cruel and ugly. She cared only about her own beauty. She wanted nothing more than to be the most beautiful person in the kingdom.

The Queen treated Snow White as if she were a servant. She cared only for her most prized possession, an enchanted mirror.

Each day she asked it, "Magic mirror on the wall, who is the fairest one of all?"

And each day the mirror answered: "*You* are the fairest one of all." This made the Queen very happy.

But one day, the mirror had a different answer:

Famed is thy beauty, Majesty,
But hold—a lovely maid I see:
Rags cannot hide her gentle grace.
Alas, she is more fair than thee.

The Queen was shocked and angry. "Who can it be? Who is fairer than I?" she cried.

"Snow White," replied the mirror.

At that very moment, Snow White was hard at work, scrubbing the stone steps in front of the castle.

"What is your name?" a deep voice suddenly asked.

Snow White jumped up in alarm. A handsome man stood beside her. He wore the rich clothes of a prince.

"I'm sorry if I scared you," he said.

Snow White was too shy to speak to the Prince. She ran inside the castle.

"Please come out," the Prince called to her. "Can't we be friends?"

Snow White peeked out at the Prince. She wanted to answer, but she was far too timid.

"I shall never forget you," the Prince declared. He leaped onto his horse. "Goodbye!" he called and galloped away.

While Snow White gazed after the stranger, the evil queen met with her huntsman.

"You will take Snow White deep into the forest," the Queen commanded. "And there you will kill her."

The huntsman turned pale. "Kill the little princess?"

The Queen turned white with rage. "Do you dare to question me?"

He bowed low. "No, Your Majesty," he murmured. "I will do as you say."

The Queen smiled to herself. Soon Snow White would no longer be alive. And the

Queen would again be the fairest in the kingdom.

The huntsman quickly found Snow White. He led her into the forest to a pretty spot filled with the wildflowers she loved. Snow White was startled when the huntsman raised his knife to strike a blow. "No!" she cried.

The huntsman dropped the weapon and fell to his knees. "Forgive me!" he cried. "I tried to obey the Queen's orders. But I cannot harm you. You must run away!"

"But where shall I go?" Snow White asked. "The castle has always been my home."

"Go anywhere!" the huntsman exclaimed. "But never, ever return!"

With fear in her heart, Snow White rushed blindly through the forest. She ran until she was too tired to run anymore. Then she fell to the ground, weeping with fright and cold, and cried herself to sleep.

The gentle morning sun awakened her. Her eyes fluttered open. She sat up and smiled in delight—a tiny rabbit was sniffing her fingers. A baby deer poked his nose into her hand. Bluebirds gathered around her. Squirrels and chipmunks came to stare at her.

Snow White spoke gently to all the animals. "I'm alone in the forest. Do you know where I could stay?"

The bluebirds twittered in reply. They flew overhead, leading Snow White deeper into the woods. The other animals followed. The forest no longer seemed such a scary place. Soon the bluebirds stopped and landed in

front of a tiny cottage.

"Is this the place? Oh, it's adorable!" Snow White exclaimed.

She knocked at the door. "Hello? May I come in?" she called. There was no answer. She gently tapped the door and it swung open.

"My goodness!" she exclaimed. "Everything is so small! These seven little chairs must belong to seven little children."

She gently touched one tiny chair. A cloud of dust flew up and tickled her nose. Snow White sneezed. "Dirt and dust everywhere!" she exclaimed.

She looked more closely around the room. "The sink is full of dirty dishes." She shook her head in dismay.

"I know what we'll do!" Snow White exclaimed. "We'll clean this cottage from top to bottom. It will be a wonderful surprise for the children!"

Snow White and the animals set to work. Snow White whistled and sang as they mopped and scrubbed and polished everything in sight.

Snow White quickly set a kettle of stew to cook over a hot fire. Then she and the animals climbed to the bedroom upstairs. It was filled wall-to-wall with seven little beds. There was a name carved into the wood at the foot of each bed.

"What funny names these children have," Snow White said as she fluffed a pillow. "Doc, Happy, Sneezy, Dopey, Bashful, Grumpy, and Sleepy." She yawned and stretched. "I'm a little sleepy myself."

Snow White lay across three of the little beds and fell fast asleep.

Across the forest, the owners of the tiny cottage were hard at work. They were seven dwarfs who dug for jewels in the mines each day. When it was time to go home they put away their tools and cheered. Then they marched across the hills to their cottage in the woods.

Ashley: I wish animals would clean our room. Then it wouldn't always be a mess!

Mary-Kate: Yeah—even a squirrel could clean better than I could!

"A light is on!" Doc cried in alarm. "We didn't leave a light burning. Someone must be inside our house!"

Doc peeked through the front door. When he didn't see anyone inside, he crept into the room.

"Why, the floor has been swept!" Doc stared in surprise.

"The windows have been washed," Sleepy added with a yawn.

"And something is cooking on the stove," Happy added.

Sneezy sniffed at the pot. "*Achoo!* It sure smells good!"

The dwarfs crept up the steps to their bedroom to search some more. There they came upon Snow White, snuggled peacefully under their covers.

"She looks like an angel!" Bashful blushed a deep, rosy red.

Snow White woke up. "Oh!" she cried, staring at the dwarfs in amazement. "You're not children after all. You're little men!" She smiled.

Grumpy frowned. "But who are *you?*"

Snow White told them about the evil queen, and how she came to live in the forest.

"Please let me stay. I will clean for you," Snow White said. Grumpy frowned. Doc shook his head.

"And I will cook for you," Snow White added.

"That does it!" Happy shouted. "She stays!"

Snow White served the Seven Dwarfs a delicious dinner. She was so cheerful and kind that she melted their hearts. Soon the little cottage was filled with music and laughter.

Snow White sang and danced and told them lots of stories. Her favorite one was about a princess who met a handsome prince. He spoke only a few words, and she spoke not at all. Still, they fell in love. The prince rode off, leaving the princess to dream of the day when he would return to her.

"I hope that princess gets to meet her prince again soon," Sleepy said with a giant yawn.

In the morning, none of the dwarfs wanted to leave Snow White.

"Please be careful," Sleepy said with a wide yawn.

"And don't let anybody into the house," Grumpy added.

Meanwhile, the Queen was happy. She believed that Snow White was dead. Alone in the castle, she gazed into her enchanted mirror. "Magic mirror on the wall, who is the fairest one of all?" she asked.

The mirror replied:

Over the seven jeweled hills
Beyond the seventh fall
In the cottage of the Seven Dwarfs
Dwells Snow White
Fairest one of all

"What! Snow White is alive?" the Queen shrieked with anger. "The huntsman tricked me!"

She raced down steep stone steps to a dungeon deep beneath the castle. "I'll have to get rid of Snow White myself!"

The wicked queen mixed a bubbling

magic potion and gulped it down. It burned her throat as it worked its spell. In a flash, the beautiful queen had become an ugly old woman, dressed in rags.

She gazed into a mirror and cackled with delight. "Snow White will never recognize me."

The Queen mixed another potion and poisoned a gleaming red apple. "One bite of this apple, and Snow White will fall under the spell of the sleeping death. A spell that can only be broken by love's first kiss!" She threw on her cloak and hurried to the cottage of the Seven Dwarfs.

All the forest animals gathered around the cottage in dismay. They knew the old woman was really the Queen! The deer and squirrels and bluebirds raced to the jewel mines to beg the dwarfs to return home.

Snow White was baking a pie. She was startled when an ugly beggar woman tapped on the window.

"Hello, my dear!" The woman grinned. "Would you like this lovely apple? Take one bite, and your dearest wish will come true."

"A magic apple!" Snow White thought of the handsome prince. She took the apple from the old woman and bit into the gleaming fruit.

In an instant, the poison did its work. Snow White fell to the floor and slept as if she were dead. The wicked queen cackled with glee and fled.

As the dwarfs ran through the forest a flash of lightning lit the sky. Grumpy spied a bent, cloaked figure sneaking away from the cottage. "The Queen!" he cried. "After her!"

The evil queen ran. The dwarfs chased her to the top of a steep, jagged cliff.

She climbed to the edge of the cliff as a giant bolt of lightning shot from the sky. It slashed the cliff in two, and the wicked queen was hurled to her death.

The dwarfs felt no joy at her death, for their beloved Snow White lay as if dead on the cold cottage floor.

They built her a beautiful coffin made of glass. Every day, they placed fresh flowers on the coffin and gazed at Snow White. They remembered the songs she sang and the stories she told. Their small hearts filled with sorrow.

The story of the fair princess who lay sleeping in a glass coffin spread far and wide. In his kingdom nearby, the handsome prince heard the story and leaped onto his white horse. He galloped

Ashley: I hate it when Snow White eats the poisoned apple.

Mary-Kate: Me, too. I always want to yell out, "Don't do it! It's the witch!"

through the deep forests until he came to the clearing where Snow White lay.

He gazed at her hair, still as black as coal—and at her skin, still as white as snow.

"It is the one I love," he declared. He thought his heart would break from sadness. He leaned over and gently placed a farewell kiss on her soft red lips. It was the kiss of true love.

Snow White's eyes fluttered open. She gazed into the face of the handsome prince.

"She's alive!" Grumpy exclaimed.

"The spell is broken!" Doc declared.

Sneezy, Dopey, Bashful, Happy, and Sleepy hugged each other and danced for joy around the happy couple.

The Prince gathered Snow White into his arms.

"You have been good, kind friends," Snow White told the Seven Dwarfs. "I shall never forget you." She kissed each of them good-bye.

The Seven Dwarfs waved farewell as Snow White and her prince rode away on his prancing white horse.

The dwarfs would miss her, but they were happy. For they knew in their hearts that Snow White's wish had come true.

Fairest-One-of-All
Enchanted Mirror

This project is enchanting! Ashley loves the jewels on this mirror the best. I think the flowers are the prettiest part. So that's why we used flowers and jewels. You can make your mirror look like ours—or come up with your own enchanting design!

You'll Need

- A plain framed mirror, square or rectangular

- A ruler

- Fabric or ribbon; about 1/3 yard

- Plastic or fabric flowers

- Plastic jewels or beads

- White glue

How to Make It

1. Use the ruler to measure each side of the mirror frame.

2. Cut the fabric into strips, 1/2 inch longer and 1/2 inch wider than each side of the frame.

3. Spread a thin layer of glue on the frame.

4. Fold under the edges of the fabric strips to create a smooth edge. Glue the fabric over the plain frame. Smooth out any wrinkles or bumps.

5. Lay flowers, jewels, and beads on top of the fabric-covered frame. When you have a design you like, glue the decorations in place. Allow the glue to dry.

6. Hang your enchanted mirror!

I love reading *The Little Mermaid* because I think Ariel is the luckiest princess of all! Wouldn't you feel lucky to live with all those beautiful fish and sea creatures?

I know I would. Sometimes, I gaze into our aquarium at home and wish that I could live inside it. It's filled with fish in every color of the rainbow. And it even has a pink underwater castle.

Sometimes I stare at that castle and dream of being a mermaid princess, just like Ariel! I could swim extra fast with a mermaid's tail. And all my friends would be beautiful sea creatures.

But wait—if I were like Ariel, I would have six mermaid sisters to play with! Now that would be fun!

Ariel really is the luckiest princess. But I wonder if she ever has trouble remembering all of her sisters' names. Can you name them all?* Try it—then have fun reading the story of the Little Mermaid.

—Mary-Kate

*Aquata, Andrina, Arista, Attina, Adella, Alana

The Little Mermaid

Once upon a time there was a beautiful little mermaid named Ariel. She had long red hair, the sparkling tail of an emerald-colored fish, and the most beautiful voice in all the sea.

Ariel's father was good King Triton. Triton loved Ariel very much, but sometimes he wished she was not so stubborn. Or so independent.

But mostly, Triton wished that Ariel was not so curious about humans. "Humans are dangerous," he warned Ariel. "They fish in the sea with sharp hooks. They try to capture sea creatures—because they want to eat them!"

"Humans can't be all bad," Ariel argued. "Maybe if you knew more about them, you'd find something to like in them."

"Never! Stay away from the surface!" the king bellowed. "Humans are evil!"

King Triton turned to Sebastian, his trusted crab advisor. "Sebastian, it's your job to watch Ariel! Make sure she stays out of trouble!"

"Yes, Your Majesty," Sebastian muttered.

"But, Father, I don't need watching," Ariel argued.

"Not another word!" the king commanded. "You are never to go to the surface again. Is that clear?"

"Yes, Father." Ariel swam unhappily away. Her best friend, Flounder, a plump little fish, saw her and raced to catch up.

"Hi, Ariel! Are we going to the surface today?" Flounder asked.

"I can't," Ariel replied. "Daddy won't let me."

"Hooray!" Flounder cheered in relief. He knew King Triton didn't want Ariel to go to the surface. And Flounder hated getting in trouble. "I guess we won't explore the ship-wreck today, either," he said.

Ariel's eyes lit up. "The shipwreck! It's not on the surface! It's on the bottom of the sea! Let's go, Flounder!"

Flounder did his best to catch up as Ariel raced to the remains of the old ship. She swam through a porthole window and searched the ship. She found two new human treasures.

One was a fork. Ariel stared. She had never seen a fork before. She lifted her other trea-

sure—a carved wooden pipe.

"Humans make such wonderful things!" Ariel exclaimed.

"But what are they?" Flounder asked.

"I don't know," Ariel admitted. "We'll have to ask Scuttle."

Scuttle was a seagull who thought he knew everything about humans. "But— Scuttle lives on the surface," Flounder pointed out. "You

promised to stay away from there."

"Daddy won't mind one quick, tiny little trip," Ariel replied.

Flounder sighed. This meant trouble, for sure! Still, he followed Ariel. They found Scuttle sunbathing on his favorite rock. Ariel handed him the fork.

Scuttle studied it. "A dinglehopper!" he exclaimed. "I haven't seen one of these in ages."

Ariel showed him the wooden pipe. "A snarfblatt!" Scuttle blew into one end. "I bet someone used to play beautiful music on this baby!"

Ariel was thrilled. "Thanks, Scuttle," she told him. She turned to Flounder. "Let's take the snarfblatt and the dinglehopper to my cave," she said.

They swam toward Ariel's secret hiding place in an underwater cave hidden behind thick bunches of seaweed. The walls of the cave were already lined with all sorts of human treasures—bottles, jewelry, even books.

Before they reached the cave, Ariel spotted Sebastian following her. She frowned.

"I am sorry, Ariel," Sebastian explained. "But you heard your father. You must stay away from the surface, from humans, from—"

"Look!" Ariel cried, interrupting Sebastian. She pointed to a huge shadow passing overhead. It was the bottom of a sailing ship headed across the ocean.

"A ship!" Ariel exclaimed. "With humans on board! I have to see it up close!" She swam quickly toward the

Mary-Kate: I would love to have a secret cave all my own.

Ashley: But you already do—our closet. It's so full of your stuff there's no room for mine!

surface of the water. Sebastian followed.

As Ariel burst through the waves, she heard the humans singing. And saw them dancing on their strange legs. How odd and clever human legs were! Ariel wondered what it would be like to walk and run and dance on legs.

"Silence, everyone!" an old man called to the dancing sailors. "It is time to wish Prince Eric happy birthday!" He bowed low before a handsome young man. "A very happy birthday to you, Eric!" he exclaimed.

Ariel stared at Prince Eric's wavy, dark hair and twinkling eyes. He was the most beautiful human she had ever seen!

"Thanks, Grimsby," Eric told the old man.

"I was hoping to be able to give you a wedding present, instead of a birthday present," Grimsby said.

Eric laughed. "I know you want me to get married. But I haven't met the right girl yet." He patted Grimsby's shoulder. "Don't worry, I'll meet her someday."

"The right girl . . . ," Ariel dreamily repeated. "If only I could marry Eric!"

No sooner had she made her wish than a crack of thunder ripped through the air. The sky turned as dark as night.

"A storm!" Grimsby shouted.

Eric's dog, Max, barked in alarm. Eric ruffled Max's long, shaggy fur. "Don't worry, Max. You'll be fine," Eric told him.

Eric and the sailors scrambled to their posts as rain poured down and huge waves lashed at the deck of the ship. A bolt of lightning struck the tall wooden mast. It burst into flames.

Soon, the whole ship was on fire.

The sailors ran for their lives. Some leaped overboard to escape the flames. No one was steering the ship. Ariel watched in horror as it smashed against the jagged rocks.

Eric and Grimsby scrambled into a lifeboat. Then Eric remembered his dog.

"Max!" Eric cried. "He's still on board!" Eric bravely dived into the raging sea. He scrambled up a rope and climbed back onto the broken ship. "Come, Max!" he called. "Jump, boy!"

Max threw himself into Eric's arms. Eric safely lifted Max into the lifeboat.

But the ship suddenly exploded in a ball of orange fire. Eric was lost from sight.

"Prince Eric!" Grimsby shouted. "Prince Eric! Where are you?"

Eric was swept into the wild ocean.

"He'll drown if I don't save him!" Ariel exclaimed. She was glad to be a mermaid as she swam after Eric. She grabbed him with one arm and pulled him along until they reached land.

Eric lay on the sandy beach without moving. Ariel didn't know if he was dead or alive! She tenderly leaned over him. He was good and kind. And so handsome. A feeling of love welled up inside her. She began to sing.

It was the most beautiful song she had ever sung, because it came from her heart.

Eric blinked in confusion. He stared up at Ariel, but she could tell he was too dazed to see her clearly.

Ariel glanced up and spotted someone approaching.

Grimsby, Eric's friend from the ship!

Ariel quickly slipped back into the ocean. She couldn't let Grimsby see her! She peeped out from behind a nearby rock.

"Who . . . ? What happened . . . ?" Eric mumbled.

"Eric! Eric, is that you?" Grimsby called as he hurried to Eric's side. "I was looking for you everywhere! Thank heaven you're safe!"

"A girl rescued me," Eric told him. "A beautiful girl. With the most beautiful voice. She sang to me, a song I'll never forget."

"Yes, yes, well, let's get you home." Grimsby flung his arms around Eric's shoulders and helped him to his castle.

Ariel watched them disappear from sight. Sebastian had seen everything.

"Come, child," he told her. "Let us go home, where we belong, under the sea."

Ariel swam along after Sebastian. But she wasn't thinking of home. She was dreaming of Eric.

He is such a dear, kind, and brave man, she thought. I love the way his hair dips over one eye. And his smile—he has such a wonderful smile.

"Ariel!" King Triton greeted her as she floated through the throne room. "I haven't seen you for hours. Come, talk with me!"

"Certainly, Father," Ariel murmured, swimming right past the king.

"What is wrong with her?" King Triton asked Sebastian.

"I think she is in love," Sebastian replied.

"In love! How wonderful!" The king chuckled.

Sebastian sighed. "I was afraid something like this would happen. I begged her to stay away from humans. I—"

"Humans!" King Triton bellowed. "What do humans have to do with it?"

Sebastian gulped. "Ariel is in love with a human named Prince Eric," he admitted. He told the king everything that had happened.

"No! Never!" the king declared. He whirled around. "Ariel! Come back here!" he ordered.

"Yes, Father?" Ariel asked.

King Triton scowled. "Is it true you saved a human from drowning?"

"I had to. He would have died!" Ariel explained.

"And that would be one less human to worry about," the king replied.

"But Daddy, I love him!" Ariel declared.

"Have you lost your senses? Ariel, I must find a way to make you listen to me!" King Triton pounded his magic trident on the floor. He vowed to destroy Ariel's human-made treasures.

Ariel burst into tears.

"I'm sorry, Ariel," King Triton turned his back and swam away.

Ariel had never felt so helpless.

Two evil eels, Flotsam and Jetsam, swam up to Ariel. They worked for Ursula, the Sea Witch.

"We can help you," Flotsam said. "We know someone who can make all your dreams come true."

"I . . . I don't understand," Ariel said.

"Ursula! She has great powers," Jetsam told her with a sly grin.

At first Ariel refused to see the witch. But she knew her father wouldn't help her.

Ariel decided to follow the slimy eels to Ursula's lair.

"Welcome," Ursula greeted them when they reached her cave. "Ariel, I would be happy to grant your wishes—for a price." She cackled.

"I will make you human for three days," Ursula went on. "Darling Prince Eric must give you the kiss of true love before the sun sets on the third day. If he does, you will remain a human—forever."

Ariel nodded eagerly.

"But if he doesn't give you the kiss, you turn back into a mermaid. And you will belong to me!" Ursula gave an evil laugh.

Ariel took a deep breath. "I . . . I agree," she said.

"Good. Oh, and one more tiny detail before you go," Ursula added. "Now I get to keep your voice."

"My . . . voice?" Ariel stared in surprise.

"That's right," Ursula replied. "You won't be able to talk or sing. But that

Mary-Kate: I couldn't stand it if I couldn't talk. I always have *something* to say!

Ashley: Yeah, but if you couldn't talk, maybe I'd finally *get* a word in!

should be no problem for a beautiful girl like you." She held out a golden scroll and a pen.

Ariel hesitated, then signed her name to the scroll.

Before the ink had dried, Ursula captured Ariel's voice and sealed it in a golden shell around her neck.

With a wave of her hand, Ursula turned Ariel's lovely tail into two human legs. Ariel could no longer breathe underwater. Sebastian and Flounder helped her swim to the ocean's surface.

Ariel swam to the beach near Eric's castle. Wearing an old piece of sail as a dress, she tried to stand on her weak, unsteady legs.

"Arf! Arf!" Max appeared and leaped at Ariel, nearly knocking her down.

"Sorry, miss! Are you all right?" Prince Eric raced to her side. He had been searching the beach for the girl who had rescued him. He still could not remember her face. But he couldn't forget her beautiful voice.

"I'm sorry if Max scared you," Eric told Ariel. He peered closely at her lovely face. "You seem familiar," Eric murmured. "What is your name?"

Ariel opened her mouth to reply. But no sound came out.

"Oh, you can't speak," Eric said in disappointment. "Then you can't possibly be the girl I'm looking for."

Yes! I am! Ariel nodded and smiled, trying to indicate that she *was* that girl.

Eric didn't understand. "Don't worry. I'll help you." He led Ariel to his castle where she was given a pretty room and a beautiful pink gown to wear. She was invited to dine with Eric and Grimsby.

Ariel was delighted with the dining room. It was filled with human treasures! Eric watched in astonishment as she lifted a fork and combed it through her hair. Then she held Grimsby's pipe to her lips and tried to play it, as if it were a flute!

Grimsby gaped at her in surprise. Ariel knew she had somehow made a mistake.

"Ahem!" Grimsby cleared his throat and suggested that Eric take Ariel on a tour throughout the kingdom. "Would you like that?" Eric asked.

Ariel nodded. She would like it very much indeed!

The next morning, Eric drove Ariel in the royal carriage over the countryside. They played at a country fair and ate a delicious picnic lunch. Eric showed her birds and flowers and trees of amazing beauty. That day and the next were filled with wonderful things to do.

Most wonderful of all was when evening came on the second day, and Eric took Ariel for a moonlit boat ride. Flounder, Scuttle, and Sebastian all waited nervously nearby. Would Eric give Ariel the kiss of true love?

But they weren't the only ones watching. Ursula had sent along her two evil eels, Flotsam and Jetsam.

Eric leaned close to Ariel in the small boat. "You're so beautiful," he murmured. "And funny, and sweet, and kind . . ."

Ariel leaned even closer, hoping for his kiss. The boat began to wobble.

Splash!

Flotsam and Jetsam tipped the boat over. Eric and Ariel plunged into the cold water. They came up laughing, but the magical moment had passed. The kiss would have to wait.

Ursula watched it all in her crystal ball. She cackled with glee. But she was worried. Eric might try to kiss Ariel again before the third day was done.

"I can't let that happen," Ursula murmured. She gulped down a magic potion. When she gazed into her mirror, she had become a lovely young girl. She stroked the locket fastened around her neck—the locket filled with Ariel's voice.

All the next day, Ariel was filled with hope. Perhaps Eric would kiss her today!

"Congratulations!" Scuttle flew through Ariel's open window. "Everyone's talking about the prince's wedding!"

The prince wanted to marry her? Ariel leaped for joy. She raced downstairs to find Eric. But he stood hand in hand with a dark-haired young woman she had never seen before.

"Congratulations on your marriage," Grimsby told the girl. "I am so pleased Eric found you, the mysterious stranger who saved his life!"

"Yes, Vanessa and I will marry today," Eric replied. "The wedding ship will depart at sunset."

No! Ariel gasped in dismay. She ran outside and flung herself onto the warm sand, weeping bitterly.

"Ariel!" Scuttle flew overhead. "I came to warn you. Vanessa is really Ursula, the Sea Witch, in disguise!"

The Sea Witch! Eric was in danger!

Ariel sent Scuttle for help. There was still time to stop the wedding—before Eric married Ursula!

Ariel reached the ship as Scuttle and his friends flew overhead. They dived at the wedding guests. They tore holes in the ship's sails.

"Stop them!" Ursula shrieked. "They're making a mess of everything!"

Max growled at Ursula. He leaped forward and bit her on the ankle.

"Yeow!" Ursula shrieked and jumped back. The locket fell to the deck and smashed apart. Ariel's voice was free! It returned to Ariel.

Ariel sang, proud and strong. The beautiful notes filled the air.

"That song," Eric murmured. He stared at Ariel. "You were the one who rescued me! You sang me that song!" Eric ran to give Ariel the kiss of true love.

Too late!

The sun slipped below the horizon. The third day had ended.

Ariel's legs disappeared. She was a mermaid again!

Ursula changed back into an octopus. She grabbed Ariel and dragged her into the sea and down to her garden of lost souls.

King Triton found them there. "Let my daughter go!" he commanded.

"Never! She is mine now," Ursula declared. She gave Triton a sly grin. "Unless *you* would like to take her place?"

"Yes!" King Triton agreed.

"Daddy, no!" Ariel cried. But Ursula had already begun her evil magic. The king turned into a twisted, quivering worm.

Ursula was reaching for Ariel when a harpoon shot through the water.

Ariel glanced up. Eric! He had come to rescue her!

Ursula glared at Eric in fury. "I am the ruler of the ocean!" she exclaimed, growing to monstrous size. "You will die!"

Ursula used King Triton's magic trident to beat the foaming water into a giant whirlpool that dragged Ariel and Eric to the bottom of the sea. The whirlpool swept up Eric's broken ship, which lay on the ocean floor. Eric jumped aboard. He steared and sent it hurtling toward Ursula. The ship's jagged mast pierced her heart like a sword. With one last scream of fury, Ursula sank to the depths of the ocean, never to be seen again. Her evil spells were broken and the lost souls in her garden were set free.

Ariel carried Eric back to land where he sprawled on the sand, barely alive.

King Triton turned to Sebastian and sighed.

"There's just one problem left," he said. "I'm going to miss Ariel so much!"

Sebastian smiled as the king approached Ariel.

"This human risked his life to save you," the king said.

"Yes," Ariel replied. "He loves me as much as I love him."

King Triton raised his mighty rod. "Ariel, I grant your wish to be human, forever!"

Ariel gasped as her mermaid's tail disappeared. In an instant, her dream came true! She was human for now and always.

Ariel awakened Eric with the kiss of true love. They were married amid joy and laughter, and Ariel and her prince lived happily ever after.

Ariel's Magical Mermaid Lampshade

Wouldn't it be fun to live under the sea? Mary-Kate and I love to see our lampshade light up! It makes us feel like we're visiting Ariel's underwater world. You can copy our designs of fish and bubbles, or find ready-made stencil designs of fish, seaweed, or seashells. Either way, you'll have oceans of fun making your own mermaid lampshade!

You'll Need

- A lamp with a white lampshade

- Fabric (enough to cover shade)

- Scissors

- Marker

- Stencils

- Glue

- Glitter paint

- Braid or ribbon trim

How to Make It

1. Roll shade along fabric to trace the shape of your shade. Cut out the fabric.

2. Trace stencil designs onto the fabric. Cut out the designs.

3. Apply glue to the fabric (avoid the cut-out areas). Press the fabric to the lampshade, smoothing out bumps and wrinkles. Let the glue dry completely.

4. Outline the cut-out shapes with glitter paint. (This will hide any rough fabric edges.) Let dry.

5. Glue fabric braid or ribbon trim to the top and bottom edges of your shade. Let dry.

No matter how many times I read Beauty and the Beast, I always think Belle is the smartest princess ever!

And she's smart in more than one way. She's definitely smart from all the things she learned in the books she's read. But she's also smart about people. She knew how to tame a scary guy like the Beast!

In the beginning of the story, I always think the Beast is creepy. I would never have the nerve to talk back to him the way Belle does! But by the end of the story, I love the Beast—because Belle teaches him to be sweet and kind.

Come to think of it, Belle is more than smart. She's brave, too! What other princess could get close enough to the Beast to put a bandage on his cuts! I wonder . . . is Belle the smartest? Or the bravest? Or both? Decide for yourself after you have fun reading Beauty and the Beast!

—Ashley

nce upon a time in a faraway land, there lived a young prince. He had everything he wanted, yet he was selfish and unkind.

One bitter-cold winter night an old beggar woman sought shelter at his castle. "I have no money," she told the prince. "I cannot pay for my meal or a warm bed. But I can give you this perfect rose."

The prince did not even glance at the rose. "Begone!" he told the woman. "You are too ugly to stay here."

"Do not judge me by my looks," the woman warned. "I am not ugly inside. And I will surely take sick if I don't stay in your warm castle tonight."

But again the prince said no.

The old woman frowned and waved her arms. The prince was astonished as she was suddenly surrounded by a shimmering, bright light. Before his eyes, she became a beautiful enchantress!

"You have no love in your heart," the enchantress angrily exclaimed. "You act no better than a beast—and so a beast you shall be!"

With a wave of her hand, she cast another spell. And the prince turned into a horrible beast. His long, waving hair grew into a shaggy mane. His gleaming white teeth turned into terrible fangs. His delicate fingers became crooked, evil-looking claws.

With a cry of terror, he turned and fled into his castle. But the enchantress followed, and cast her spell over the entire castle. The prince watched in fear as everything around him changed.

His loyal butler, Cogsworth, was turned into a ticking clock. Lumiere, another servant, became a candlestick. The housekeeper, Mrs. Potts, became a teapot. Her young son, Chip, turned into a chipped china cup. Not one human being was left in the castle.

"To break the spell, you must learn to love someone," the enchantress told the Beast. "Someone who must love you in return." She handed him the perfect red rose. "This rose will bloom until your twenty-first birthday. If you cannot break the spell by then, it will be too late. You shall remain a Beast forever!"

"I cannot bear my own ugliness!" the Beast exclaimed. "I will never leave the castle." He shuddered.

"Then take this magic mirror," the enchantress replied. "You can use it to view the outside world."

"Why would I want to see the world outside?" the Beast asked. "I am a monster. I will never find anyone to love, or to love me."

"As you wish!" The enchantress waved her arms and disappeared.

The Beast glanced in the mirror and howled with rage. How would he ever escape the powerful spell?

Not far from the Beast's castle there lived a girl named Belle. She was beautiful—the most beautiful girl in her village. But she was unlike the other village girls, because she loved to read. She read stories about exciting people and places—stories that were far more exciting than the dull and quiet life of the village.

Her father, Maurice, also thought the village dull. He was an inventor. His latest invention was a machine that chopped firewood.

"Belle, come look!" Maurice cried in excitement. "My woodchopper is finally running! Just in time to take it to the fair in the next village."

Belle gazed at the machine in admiration. "It's a wonderful invention," Belle told him. "I'm sure you'll win first prize at the fair." She helped Maurice hitch their horse, Phillipe, to his wagon.

"Wish me luck!" Maurice called as Phillipe trotted off.

Maurice was a wonderful inventor. But he was not a wonderful driver. In a short time, he became hopelessly lost. He and Phillipe shuddered with fear as the woods around them grew dark.

Suddenly a pack of wolves appeared. Phillipe reared in fright and Maurice tumbled from his seat. "Phillipe! Come back!" Maurice called. But the frightened horse galloped away leaving Maurice behind.

Maurice ran in terror. The hungry wolves nipped at his heels. He spied a huge iron gate and squeezed through, leaving the wolves behind. Ahead of him

was a dark, spooky castle—the castle of the Beast. Maurice shivered with fear. He would have turned and fled, but a storm was brewing. Maurice hurried to seek shelter inside the castle.

But there was no storm approaching the village. Belle sat happily on a bench outside her house, reading her book. She paid no attention to the crowd that gathered around her. She didn't even notice Gaston, the tall, strong, handsome man who stood in the center of the crowd, showing off his muscles.

"Belle!" Gaston finally cried. "Put down that silly book! You'll be late to our wedding!"

Belle looked up in surprise. "Gaston! What are you talking about? What wedding? You know I refused to marry you!"

Gaston frowned. "But I am so handsome! Of course you want to marry me. Who wouldn't?"

"Me," she muttered under her breath. "No, Gaston," she said. "We can't be married."

Gaston was furious. "I will have you for my wife," he vowed. Gaston turned on his heels. He strode angrily away just as Phillipe, the horse, returned to the house alone.

"Phillipe!" Belle cried in alarm. "Where's Papa? Take me to him!"

Phillipe led Belle through the dark forest to the iron gate hidden in the woods. Belle spotted Maurice's hat lying on the ground. With a cry of fear, she snatched it up. She ran through the heavy gate and up to the castle. She pushed open the doors and slipped inside to search for her father.

She shivered as she hurried through the cold, empty rooms. She climbed high into a stone tower. There she heard someone coughing. "Papa?" she cried, rushing to a locked door. She peered through the window. "Is that you?"

"Belle!" Her father pulled himself up to the window, coughing. "You must leave here! This place is ruled by a terrible beast! He has locked me in this cell!"

Roaaaarrrr! A huge creature leaped out of the shadows. It was the Beast.

"You don't belong here!" the Beast snarled at Belle.

Belle gathered every ounce of her courage to face the terrible Beast. "My father is sick!" she declared. "You must let him go. If you want a prisoner, take me instead."

The Beast gazed at Belle's lovely face. "You may stay," he answered. "If you promise to remain here forever."

Belle took a deep breath. "I promise," she replied.

Maurice was set free and the Beast led Belle into a pretty bed-

Ashley: Do you think Gaston is really in love with Belle?

Mary-Kate: No— He's in love with himself! And that's scary!

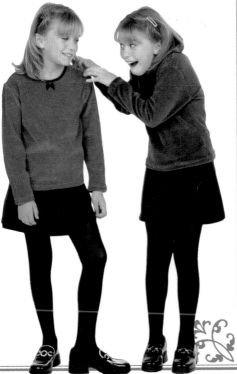

room. "This will be your room," he told her. "You may go anywhere in the castle—except the West Wing. The West Wing is forbidden!"

Belle shuddered at the Beast's harsh voice.

"And tonight, you will have dinner with me," he commanded.

"No!" Belle told him. "I won't!"

"Then go hungry!" The Beast roared in anger and locked Belle inside her room.

Belle felt her heart sink. Perhaps Father will come back and save me, she thought. She lay on her bed and wept.

Tap, tap, tap. The door opened and Belle stared in astonishment as Mrs. Potts came in with her son, Chip.

A teapot serving tea? Belle stared in wonder. Mrs. Potts and Chip were so warm and friendly that Belle was not in the least bit afraid.

Finally, Belle thought, I'm having a real adventure! Just like the adventures I've read about in my books!

Belle gulped down her tea. She felt much better—and also very hungry. Beast or no Beast, she needed food.

Mrs. Potts showed Belle the way to the kitchen. The enchanted servants, Cogsworth and Lumiere, served her a fabulous meal.

"Everyone here is so friendly," Belle said. Everyone but the Beast, she added to herself. "Could I see the rest of the castle?" she asked.

"We'd be delighted," Cogsworth exclaimed.

"We'll show you everything," Lumiere added. He hoped Belle could somehow break the spell that kept the servants and the castle enchanted. He and Cogsworth led Belle everywhere—except into the forbidden West Wing.

Belle could not control her curiosity. She had never been inside any castle before, much less an enchanted castle! The moment Cogsworth and Lumiere were out of sight, Belle slipped into the West Wing. She had to find out what the Beast was hiding there.

The West Wing was darker and gloomier than the rest of the castle. No one had lived in these rooms for a very long time.

In one room, Belle found a perfect red rose under a glass dome. She had to touch it! As she reached out her hand, the Beast leaped out from the shadows.

"I told you never to come here!" the Beast roared. "Now get out!"

In terror, Belle raced down the stairs. "Promise or no promise, I can't stay here!" she declared.

She found the loyal Phillipe waiting outside and jumped on his back. "Take me home!" she cried.

They galloped past the castle grounds and into the dark woods. The hungry wolves gave

chase. Belle tried to fight them, but it was no use. There were too many. The wolves bared their fangs and attacked poor Belle.

Roaaarrrr! The Beast appeared. He lashed out at the wolves and saved Belle. The wolves ran off. But the Beast was horribly injured. He fell to the ground with a moan of pain, lying wounded in the snow.

Belle didn't know what to do. The Beast couldn't catch her now. She could escape. But he saved her life. She couldn't leave him alone to die.

She leaned over him. "Try to stand up," she told him. "I will help you back to the castle."

Belle half-carried the Beast back inside the warm castle, where she tended his wounds. "I never thanked you for saving my life," she said.

The Beast gazed at her in wonder. No one had ever thanked him for anything before. "You're welcome," he answered in the first gentle words he had ever spoken.

Belle looked at him in surprise. He didn't seem so frightening anymore.

From that moment on, the Beast began to speak without shouting. He began to play and to have fun. He began to know what it was like to care for animals—and for another person. For the first time in his life, he was happy.

Belle found that beneath his ragged fur the Beast was gentle and thoughtful and kind. Kind enough to be a true friend. She liked him more and more each day. One night the Beast planned a special evening. He dressed in his finest clothes. Belle wore a shimmering gown of gold. She thought the Beast looked handsome in his dashing dark suit. They shared a delicious dinner and laughed and talked about their favorite books.

Then they whirled around the beautiful ballroom, dancing for hours.

"Belle, are you happy here?" the Beast asked.

"Oh, yes!" Belle replied. It was true. "Except—I miss my father," she admitted.

"I can show him to you," said the Beast. He handed Belle the magic mirror. Belle glanced into its shiny surface and saw her father. He seemed terribly ill.

"It's Papa!" she cried. "He's sick! He may be dying!" she told the Beast. "I must go to him!"

"You want to leave here?" The Beast felt a pang of sadness. He was growing to love Belle. He hoped she might love him—and break the spell that kept him a beast.

"I must," Belle said. "Papa needs me!"

"Then I release you," the Beast replied. "Find your father," he said. He handed her the magic mirror. "But take this mirror, so you'll have a way to remember me," he added.

"Thank you so much!" Belle cried. She kissed his paw and flew from the ballroom.

Sadly, the Beast watched Belle leave. He hadn't realized how much he loved her until she had gone. But did Belle love him? He would never know.

Soon, it would be his twenty-first birthday. The enchanted rose would die. And he would remain a beast forever.

As Belle hurried through the forest, she glanced again into her magic mirror. She saw Maurice.

He shouted as he ran through the village. "The Beast has taken Belle prisoner!"

"What beast?" The villagers laughed in his face. "Maurice, you're crazy," they said.

"Then I'll rescue her myself!" he exclaimed. Belle saw Maurice run toward the forest. But he was so tired and ill that he could not go on. He collapsed in a heap.

With the help of the Beast's magic mirror, Belle soon found him. "Father!" she cried, running to his side. "Let me help you." She led him back to their cottage and put him to bed.

"Hello!" chirped a little voice.

Belle whirled in surprise. "Chip!" The little teacup had hidden himself in her bag at the castle. Now he hopped out, smiling.

"A stowaway!" Belle laughed, delighted to see Chip again. She wanted to talk with him about the Beast. Belle missed him more than she imagined she would. But at that moment there was a loud pounding on the door.

"Let us in!" voices roared.

Belle flung the door open. A crowd of villagers rushed up. "We heard about Maurice. He's crazy," they shouted. "He says he saw a beast!"

"My father isn't crazy!" Belle exclaimed.

Gaston stepped forward. "Don't worry, Belle," he told her. "I'll tell them your father isn't crazy—*if* you agree to marry me!"

"Never!" Belle declared.

Gaston shrugged. "Then I'll let the villagers take your father away," he warned. "They'll throw him in a terrible place—a place where crazy people are left to suffer!"

"But I can prove there *is* a beast," Belle insisted. She snatched up the magic mirror. "Show the Beast!" she ordered. The mirror glowed and an image of the Beast appeared. Belle held it up for all the crowd to see.

The crowd drew back in fright.

"Don't be scared," Belle said quickly. "This Beast isn't mean at all. He's kind, and gentle. He's my friend!"

Gaston saw the love in Belle's eyes. He felt a burst of jealousy. Belle, in love with a beast! Belle, who refused to marry him?

Gaston grabbed the mirror away. "The Beast is evil," he told the villagers. "He is dangerous! We must kill him!" Gaston locked Belle and her father in the cellar.

"No!" Belle shouted. But it was no use. The villagers believed Gaston. "Kill the Beast!" the villagers roared. They marched to the castle.

Belle had to save the Beast! But how could they escape the cellar?

At that moment, Chip was walking around Maurice's large wood-chopping machine. He turned a few knobs, gave it a nudge . . . and it rolled down the hill, crashing into the cellar door! Belle and Maurice were free!

Belle grabbed Chip and fetched Phillipe. "Take us to the castle!" she cried. She leaped onto the faithful horse and they galloped through the forest. When they reached the castle, Gaston and the villagers had already broken inside.

But they weren't expecting to fight an enchanted castle!

Lumiere and Cogsworth poured hot tea over them. The

dishes flew through the air and shattered over their heads. Chairs and chests of drawers leaped and jumped and slammed into them. The kitchen knives attacked them. The village men fled the castle in terror.

But Gaston would not leave until he had slain the Beast. The Beast watched as Gaston drew back his bow and aimed a deadly arrow.

The Beast made no move to defend himself. He did not wish to live if Belle did not love him.

Gaston let his arrow fly. The Beast cried out in pain. He was wounded.

"Gaston, no!" Belle shouted. "Please, don't hurt him!"

At the sound of her voice, the Beast swung around in surprise. Belle's worried eyes were full of love. Belle loved him!

The Beast no longer wanted to die. With a mighty roar, he sprang at Gaston and wrestled with him at the edge of the castle roof.

"Don't kill me!" Gaston begged.

The Beast felt so much love in his heart for Belle that he could not hate even Gaston!

"I feel sorry for you," the Beast said. He set Gaston down and turned away.

Gaston drew a knife and stabbed the Beast in the back. "No!" Belle shouted in horror.

Gaston leaped at the Beast to stab him again. But he lost his balance and plunged off the roof to his death.

Belle kneeled at the Beast's side. "Please don't die," she begged. "Don't ever leave me!"

"At least I got to see you one last time," the Beast replied.

Belle felt as though her heart would break. "I love you," she whispered.

At that moment, the last petal of the enchanted rose fell to the ground. The Beast closed his eyes for the last time. All was quiet except for the soft sound of Belle's weeping.

Then sparks of light began to rain down upon them.

The lights grew brighter. As Belle watched in amazement, the Beast began to change. His paws became human hands and feet.

His back straightened and his rough fur and pointed fangs and horns shrank and disappeared. In place of the Beast was a handsome young prince.

The prince opened his deep blue eyes. "Belle!" he cried with joy.

Belle stared at him in confusion. "But—who are you?" she asked. Then, in the prince's eyes, she saw the same kindness and love that she had seen in the eyes of the Beast.

"It *is* you!" she exclaimed.

The spell was broken. The prince's enchanted servants gathered around. They changed before her eyes. Cogsworth, Lumiere, Mrs. Potts, and Chip became human once again.

"I don't understand," Belle cried. She listened, astonished, as the Prince told his story. He explained how he was punished for not having love in his heart.

"Thanks to you, my heart is full of love," he told Belle.

"As is mine." Belle smiled and embraced him.

And the beautiful Belle and her prince lived happily ever after.

Ashley: I love the happy ending when Belle and the Beast discover they love each other.

Mary-Kate: I know it's a happy ending, but why does it always make me cry?

Perfectly Beautiful Red Red Rose

Ashley and I love having flowers around. We made this rose using an ancient Japanese method of folding paper. It's called origami. At first, we didn't believe we could make a beautiful rose from a plain piece of paper. But we did. And the best part is, it will never need watering!

You'll Need

- 8-1/2 x 8-1/2 square of red construction paper

- Green pipe cleaners or green construction paper

- Stapler

How to Make It

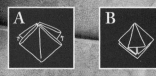

1. Mark one side of the paper with a small X. With the marked side up, fold the square in half and make a crisp crease. Unfold.

2. Fold and crease the paper from the opposite direction to make a cross. Flip the paper over to the unmarked side.

3. Fold the unmarked side in half diagonally, so that the corners meet. Unfold.

4. Now fold and crease the paper diagonally from the opposite direction. You now have a beginning model of your rose. Flip the model over to the marked side again. (To see if you have done everything correctly so far, place your finger in the center of the model and push down—all four corners should pop up into the air.)

5. Lift the four corners of your model together so they meet in the center. There will be four flaps extending from the center. (Picture A)

6. Flatten the model into a square with two flaps on the left and two flaps on the right. Lift one top flap and push on the folded edge, creating a cone shape. Flatten the cone shape, creating a triangle. (Picture B)

7. Repeat Step 6 with the remaining flaps. You should now have four small flaps on each side.

8. Fold down the pointed top to expose the two half-triangles beneath. Crease. (Picture C) Turn the flap and repeat this step.

9. With a folded small triangle flap facing you (as in Picture D), fold all the thickness of the cone down from the right top corner, on the diagonal. (Picture D) Crease. Repeat this step from the opposite side.

10. Hold your model and fold away from you. Crease in the center. (See dotted line, Picture E.)

11. Holding the bottom of your flower, pull the outermost flaps toward each other and away from you. (Picture F)

12. Finally, place your thumb at the end of each petal and gently fold down the corners to round out your petals. (Picture G)

13. Shape green pipe cleaners into a stem shape, or cut a stem shape from a piece of green construction paper. Staple the bottom of the flower to the stem.

Hold on to your magic carpet, it's time to read about Jasmine, the most magical princess to soar through the sky.

After I read the story of Aladdin, I had one wish—to fly on a magic carpet just the way Jasmine did.

My grandma had a little rug that looked just like Aladdin's magic carpet. One day I pulled it in front of a big fan and sat down. Then I lifted one end and tried to make the fan blow air under it. I thought the air would lift the carpet right off the ground. I sat there wishing and wishing that it would take off. But it didn't.

I guess it was just the wrong kind of carpet. But it's still fun to pretend that I might find the right kind of carpet someday! I'd take Ashley on a ride to Agrabah, the city where Jasmine and Aladdin lived. It sounds like the most magical place on earth.

Read Aladdin and see if you agree!

—Mary-Kate

Aladdin

Once upon a time, in the country of Persia, in the city of Agrabah, there lived a young man named Aladdin. Aladdin was poor and had no family. People called him a street rat and a thief.

"I'm not a street rat," Aladdin told his little monkey, Abu. "And I don't like to steal. But we need to eat, don't we? And we don't have money to buy our food." Abu nodded in agreement.

Aladdin gazed out over Agrabah. In the distance he saw the huge, golden domes of the sultan's palace.

"I bet nobody in the palace ever goes hungry," Aladdin told Abu. "I wish I was as rich as the sultan. Then I'd never steal food anymore. And that means I'd never have to worry about the sultan's guards. Because they chase me everywhere I go! They make me feel trapped!"

Abu pointed to the marketplace. Aladdin laughed. "Has my talk of food made you hungry? Come, let's go!"

Aladdin and Abu hurried through the crowded streets. Aladdin gave one more longing glance at the sultan's palace.

Deep inside the palace was someone who also felt trapped—the sultan's daughter, Jasmine.

Princess Jasmine was the most beautiful maiden in the whole kingdom. The law declared that she must marry before her next birthday—only three days away.

Many princes begged for Jasmine's hand in marriage. But Jasmine turned down every one of them.

Her father was angry. "The law says you must marry a prince!" he told her.

"I don't care," Jasmine replied. "When I marry, it will be for love—not because of a foolish law!"

The sultan adored his daughter, but he stamped his foot in frustration. "Jasmine, you must obey," he wailed.

Jasmine scowled as her father marched away. She pulled on a billowing cloak and kissed her pet tiger, Rajah, good-bye. "I'm going to see what life is like outside these walls," she told him. "I want to taste the freedom of those who are not royal."

Jasmine climbed over the garden wall and rushed into the crooked streets of Agrabah. She strode quickly through the marketplace, drinking in the sights and sounds. She noticed a child gazing hungrily at an apple cart.

She picked up an apple and handed it to him. "Here you go," she said.

"I hope you can pay for that," the fruit seller snarled. "There are laws against stealing!"

"But the child is hungry," Jasmine protested.

"I can't help that," the fruit seller growled. "The penalty for stealing is to lose a hand!" He seized Jasmine's wrist and raised his knife.

Jasmine cried out in fear and surprise.

Aladdin was nearby and saw what happened. He grabbed Jasmine's hand. "Run!" he cried.

"Stop, thieves!" the fruitseller shouted. "I'll send the sultan's guards after you!"

Aladdin and Jasmine raced to his crumbling rooftop home.

"Is this really where you live?" Jasmine asked in disbelief. The bare roof was very different from her rich rooms at the palace.

"It's not much, but it has a great view," Aladdin joked. He nodded at the palace in the distance. It shone like a jewel in the night. "Wouldn't it be great to live there?"

"Where everyone tells you how to act?" Jasmine replied. "You could never make your own choices," Jasmine told him.

"But I feel trapped here," Aladdin said.

"I also feel trapped," Jasmine said.

Aladdin grinned. "We have a lot in common!"

At that moment, the sultan's guards burst onto the rooftop. "There he is! There's the street rat!" the head guard cried. "Seize him!"

The guards grabbed Aladdin.

"Unhand him," Jasmine commanded. She threw back her hood to reveal herself. "By order of the princess!"

"The princess?" Aladdin stared at her in shock.

"It's true," Jasmine admitted. "I ran away because my father wanted to force me to marry a prince. That is the rule. But I do not want to obey it!"

"I am sorry, your highness." The head guard drew himself up to his full height. "But my orders come from Jafar. I must arrest Aladdin."

Jasmine frowned. Of all the men who worked for her father, Jafar had the most power. He knew how to cast magic spells. And the sultan trusted him. Jasmine could do nothing against Jafar.

The guards chained Aladdin's wrists together and dragged him to the palace, where they threw him into a prison cell.

Aladdin barely thought about being in prison. All he could think about was Jasmine. She was a beautiful princess, who also hated rules—she was wonderful! He wanted to speak to her again. He wanted to learn everything about her.

Aladdin lay in the dark, cold cell, dreaming of Jasmine's lovely face. Abu appeared at the tiny window.

"Abu—what took you so long?" Aladdin chuckled as Abu squeezed between the iron bars that covered the window and dropped down into Aladdin's cell.

Aladdin held out his chained wrists. "Get me out of these," he said.

Abu picked open the lock and the heavy chains dropped to the floor.

"Good boy, Abu!" Aladdin rubbed his sore wrists. "Now, let's get away from this place!"

"Wait!" An old beggar man stepped out of the shadows. It was Jafar, in disguise. "Would you like to be rich beyond your wildest dreams?" he asked. "All you need is a magic lamp!"

The old man explained that he knew where to find such a lamp. But he was too weak to make the journey alone. Aladdin was young and strong. If Aladdin would agree to help, the old man would share the lamp's treasures with him. He didn't admit his true reason for needing Aladdin's help—he knew that finding the lamp would be very, very dangerous!

"I knew I'd be rich someday!" Aladdin exclaimed to Abu. He turned to the old man. "Show me the way," he said.

The old man led Aladdin and Abu deep into the desert. Just when Aladdin felt too hot and tired to go on, the old man stopped. He chanted a magic spell. As Aladdin stared in awe, an enormous tiger's head rose out of the desert sand.

The tiger began to speak. "You may enter," it boomed. "But be warned! Once inside, touch nothing but the lamp!"

Aladdin strode through the tiger's mouth and into the Cave of Wonders, a vast room filled with treasures. Towers of gold coins and heaps of sparkling jewels dazzled his eyes.

Aladdin gaped in amazement as a flying carpet sprang up in front of him. He followed the carpet through the treasure room. He caught sight of an old, dull metal lamp sitting on top of a stone altar.

"Could this old lamp really be magic?" Aladdin frowned. The lamp was dusty and dented. "What should I do, Abu?" he asked.

Abu made a face at the lamp. He reached out and grabbed a huge, gleaming ruby. "Abu! No!" Aladdin yelled.

"He has touched the forbidden treasure!" the tiger roared. "Now you shall be punished!"

The walls of the cave began to tremble.

The ceiling shuddered and shook.

"Help!" Aladdin cried to the old man.

"Give me the lamp!" he yelled in reply.

Aladdin tossed him the lamp. The old man tucked it inside his cloak and ran from the cave. The mouth to the cave slammed shut. Aladdin was trapped!

Aladdin blinked in surprise. The cave was no longer filled with riches. It had become a dark, empty space.

"I don't know what just happened," Aladdin told Abu. "But I do know that old man was no friend. Now he's gone—with the magic lamp."

Abu grinned. He reached inside his vest and pulled out—the lamp!

"Why, you little thief! You stole it back!" Aladdin grasped the lamp and studied it. "There's something written here. But the lamp is too dirty to read the words." He rubbed it with his sleeve and the magic lamp began to glow.

Blue smoke poured out of its spout. The smoke swirled and twirled and took the form of an enormous blue man—a genie! The Genie turned to Aladdin with a grateful smile. "You set me free. So you win three wishes—and no wishing for more wishes. That's the rule."

"You have to follow rules?" Aladdin glanced at Abu and winked. "He isn't a very powerful genie. He probably can't even get us out of this cave!"

"Oh, no?" The Genie was greatly offended. "Watch this!" He scooped up Aladdin, Abu,

and the flying carpet and blasted them through the roof of the cave.

They streaked across the sky like a comet and landed in a splendid oasis —a desert paradise, where a pond of cool, delicious water was surrounded by swaying palm trees.

"Okay. You used up one of your wishes," the Genie told Aladdin. "That's one down, two to go."

"I never wished to get us out of the cave," Aladdin pointed out. "You did that on your own."

"Right!" The Genie looked at Aladdin with new respect. "You are clever, Master. But no more freebies."

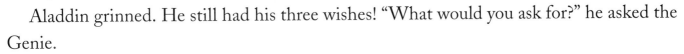

Mary-Kate: If you had a genie, what would you wish for?

Ashley: I'd wish for a horse. No, another dog. No, wait—a new computer. Oh, I don't know what I'd wish for!

Mary-Kate: Maybe you should wish you could make up your mind!

Aladdin grinned. He still had his three wishes! "What would you ask for?" he asked the Genie.

"That's easy," the Genie answered. "I would wish to be free. I may have amazing powers, but I'm also trapped. I am forever a prisoner of the lamp."

Aladdin was thoughtful. "I know how it feels to be trapped," he said. "After you grant my first two wishes, I'll use my third wish to set you free. I promise."

The genie eagerly agreed to the bargain.

Aladdin had to choose his first wish. He thought about Princess Jasmine, trapped back in her palace. She would soon be forced to marry a prince. A prince she did not love.

"That's it!" Aladdin shouted with glee. "Genie, I have my wish! I want you to make me a prince!"

"All right!" the Genie replied.

Instantly, Aladdin's rags changed into the finest silk. A jeweled turban appeared on his head. Next, the Genie turned Abu into a handsome elephant for Aladdin to ride on.

"Take me to the royal palace," Aladdin ordered the elephant. In no time, they were there. But Aladdin found things had changed while he was gone. Jafar had used his evil magic to put the sultan under a spell.

"Now I control you!" Jafar told the sultan. "You will order Princess Jasmine to marry me!"

The sultan turned to Jasmine. "Daughter, I order you to—"

"Wait!" Aladdin shouted. "I, Prince Ali Ababwa, have come to seek Jasmine's hand in marriage! I am the one who will win her heart."

"How dare you!" Jasmine cried. "I am not some prize to be won!"

"Don't be so hasty," the sultan told her. He was delighted with Prince Ali Ababwa.

But Jafar wasn't pleased. "I don't trust this prince," he murmured to the sultan.

Aladdin stared closely at Jafar and gasped in surprise. He recognized Jafar as the old man! Jafar had disguised himself, then tricked Aladdin into finding the magic lamp. Jafar wanted the lamp—and the Genie—for himself.

Luckily, Jafar did not recognize Aladdin. Aladdin's eyes narrowed. He vowed not to let Jafar trick him again.

That night, Aladdin hid the magic lamp under his turban. Then he rode the flying carpet to Jasmine's balcony. He convinced her to go for a magic carpet ride around the world.

Jasmine was dazzled by tall mountains and wild rivers and cities more magnificent than any she had ever seen.

When the carpet returned to the palace, Jasmine turned to Aladdin in excitement. "That was the most wonderful ride I ever had!" she exclaimed. "I felt trapped my whole life. But I don't feel trapped now!"

"I feel free, too," Aladdin agreed.

"You know, Prince Ali," Jasmine went on, "It's too bad Abu didn't come with us."

"Oh, he doesn't really like flying," Aladdin answered.

"I knew it!" Jasmine's eyes flashed. "You're Aladdin! Why did you pretend to be a prince?"

Aladdin wanted to tell Jasmine the truth. But he was afraid. He knew a princess could only marry a prince— not a street rat!

"I . . . I really am a prince," he told her. "I just pretended to be an ordinary person. Like you," he added. "The day I met you in the marketplace, you were doing the very same thing!"

"That's true," Jasmine replied. "I'm sorry I was angry. Thank you for the wonderful ride!" Jasmine gave Aladdin a sweet kiss good night.

Aladdin was bursting with happiness as he left the palace. He felt as if he could fly without a magic carpet! But his happiness faded as Jafar suddenly appeared, surrounded by the sultan's guards.

"Seize him!" Jafar ordered. "Take him away. And make sure he is never found. That way, he'll never marry the princess!"

The guards tied Aladdin with strong ropes and threw him into the sea. But Aladdin quickly summoned the Genie, who freed him.

In a flash, Aladdin was back inside the palace.

"You'd better get out of here, Jafar!" Aladdin told him. "Or I'll have the Genie take care of you!"

But Jafar used his magic first. *Poof!* In an instant, he disappeared in a puff of smoke.

The next morning, Jafar's parrot, Iago, stole the lamp from Aladdin. Later that day, Jasmine and Aladdin joined the sultan on the grand balcony overlooking the town square.

"People of Agrabah," the sultan began. "My daughter, Princess Jasmine, has chosen to marry Prince Ali Ababwa!"

At that moment, Jafar appeared, rubbing the magic

lamp. Out popped the Genie. "Grant me my first wish. I will be the sultan!" Jafar cried.

"Genie, stop him!" Aladdin commanded.

"Sorry, Aladdin. I can no longer obey you," the Genie replied. "Jafar has the magic lamp. He is my new master."

Jafar made his second wish. "I wish to be the most powerful sorcerer in the world!"

"Goodbye, Aladdin—and good riddance!" Jafar cackled. Jafar used his magic to send Aladdin, Abu, and the flying carpet high into a palace tower. Then he sent the tower hurtling into space like a rocket.

The tower landed in the middle of a snowstorm. Aladdin and Abu were thrown into the snow. But they quickly leaped onto the carpet. "Take us back to Agrabah!" Aladdin commanded.

They arrived to find Jasmine and the sultan in chains.

"Now you have to be my queen," Jafar told Jasmine.

"Never!" Jasmine cried. "I love another!"

Jafar rubbed the magic lamp. "For my next wish, make Jasmine fall in love with me," he commanded.

"No!" Aladdin tried to attack Jafar. But Jafar imprisoned Jasmine in a giant hourglass. Sand poured down upon her. She would be buried alive!

"Are you afraid to fight me?" Aladdin yelled at Jafar. "You are a cowardly snake!"

"A snake, am I?" Jafar shrieked. Instantly, he became an enormous cobra with glowing red eyes and poisonous fangs. He seized Aladdin and squeezed him.

"This is the end for you, street rat!" Jafar declared. "You can't defeat the most powerful sorcerer on earth!"

"You're not so powerful!" Aladdin replied. "The Genie has more power than you!"

That stopped Jafar. "You're right," he said. He grabbed the magic lamp. "Genie, I command you—make me an all-powerful genie!"

The Genie chuckled. "You asked for it," he muttered.

Jafar turned bright red and grew to an enormous size. Gold chains clamped around his wrists.

"Wait—what's happening?" Jafar asked. Suddenly, he was sucked into a metal lamp. "Oh, no!" he shrieked.

"You wished to be a genie," Aladdin calmly told him. "And genies live in lamps! Now begone!"

The Genie sent Jafar's metal lamp flying far, far into the desert. "That's the last we'll see of him," he said.

Aladdin broke the hourglass and freed Jasmine. She rushed into his arms.

"Master, you still have one wish left," the Genie told Aladdin. "Say the word and you're a prince again."

"No thanks, Genie," Aladdin replied. He turned to Jasmine. "I'm not really a prince," he admitted. "But I like being who I am." He turned to the Genie. "I didn't forget my promise," he said. "With my last wish, I set you free."

"Free at last!" The Genie leaped for joy. "Aladdin, you'll always be a prince of a guy to me!"

The sultan happily agreed. "Jasmine was right," he declared. "Our old law was foolish. From this day forth, we will have a new law! The princess shall wed whomever she chooses."

"I like this new rule." Jasmine beamed. She pointed to Aladdin. "And I choose him!"

The next day, Jasmine and Aladdin were married. They were finally free—to love each other and to live happily ever after.

Magic
Genie
Surprise Bottle

What could be better than
finding a genie bottle and
having wishes come true?
We may not be genies, but
we love making our friends'
wishes come true. That's
why we thought of this cool
craft idea—genie bottles
with surprise wishes inside!
Make one for all your
special friends.

You'll Need

- Colored tissue paper

- A small plastic bottle, such as a soda or water bottle (or, you can buy one in a craft shop like we did)

- White glue

- Glitter glue

- String

- A piece of writing paper

How to Make It

1. Cut out triangles, diamonds, and square shapes from the colored tissue paper.

2. Cover your bottle with a thin layer of white glue.

3. Glue the tissue paper shapes onto the bottle. Cover the bottle completely with your shapes.

4. Using the glitter glue, outline each tissue paper shape with a line of glue about 1/4 inch thick.

5. Use more glitter glue to decorate the mouth of the bottle.

6. Write your friend a special "wish-come-true" message on the piece of paper. (Some sample messages: "I promise to help you clean your room!" or "I promise to play your favorite game with you—three times!")

7. Roll up the "wish-come-true" message and tie one end of the string around it to keep it tightly rolled.

8. Carefully slip the rolled-up message into the bottle. Leave the long end of the string hanging out the top of the bottle.

Are you ready to read the story of Pocahontas? I am—and I can't wait!

Pocahontas is amazing. She can do everything! She's really strong and she's really brave. She dives off high cliffs. She runs as fast as the wind. And she can even move through the forest without making a sound!

I tried to move like that once. I wanted to sneak up behind Mary-Kate without her knowing I was there. But it was really, really hard. First, I tried to tiptoe through a puddle, but I made a great big splash!

Then I tried to walk over some leaves, but they were so crunchy and noisy they made me jump! Not making a sound isn't as easy as it looks. Maybe I should have tried it barefoot, like Pocahontas—the most courageous princess of all!

—Ashley

Pocahontas

 ong ago, an Indian maiden named Pocahontas lived a peaceful life near the banks of a gentle river. One day, there was great rejoicing in her village. Her father, Chief Powhatan, and his braves were returning home from a long hunting trip.

"Father!" Pocahontas ran to embrace him. "Welcome home!"

"I missed you, my daughter," Chief Powhatan told her. "Did you have any troubles while I was gone?"

"Only a puzzling dream," Pocahontas replied. "It told me that something surprising would soon happen to me."

"Your dream is true," Powhatan replied. "My bravest warrior, Kocoum, has asked for your hand in marriage."

"Marry Kocoum?" Pocahontas tossed her head. "Oh, Father, I do not want to marry him. Kocoum is far too serious for me! Besides, I believe I have another path to follow."

Powhatan gave her a stern look. "Pocahontas, you are brave and independent. But it is time for you to take your place among our people—you shall be Kocoum's bride." The chief strode away.

Pocahontas's friend, Meeko, a small raccoon, leaped from a tree to land at her feet.

"Oh, Meeko!" Pocahontas cried in dismay. "What shall I do? This is a problem I cannot solve alone. But Grandmother Willow will know what I should do!"

Pocahontas and Meeko traveled along a stream until they reached a shady glade. There stood Grandmother Willow, the tallest, oldest willow tree in the forest.

Pocahontas believed that spirits could live anywhere—some spirits lived in people, some lived in trees. Grandmother Willow had a spirit that was very old and very wise.

"Grandmother Willow, I need your help," Pocahontas called to the tree. "Tell me—how will I know what path to follow?"

A face seemed to appear in the gnarled tree trunk—Grandmother Willow's face. "All around you are spirits," she replied. "You must listen to them with your heart as well as your ears. Then you will understand."

Pocahontas closed her eyes. "I hear the wind," she murmured. "It says clouds are coming. Strange clouds!"

Pocahontas climbed high into Grandmother Willow's branches. Far away, on the glittering water, she saw the white billowing sails of a sailing ship.

"Meeko, look!" Pocahontas exclaimed. "Strange clouds!"

When she returned to the village she learned that her people had also seen the strange-looking clouds.

"The clouds are the sails of a great ship," Powhatan explained. He called a meeting with all his warriors. "Who are these strangers?" he asked.

"I fear they are not men, like us," answered Kekata, the medicine man. "I fear they are like wolves, eating everything in their path."

Kocoum jumped to his feet. "Then I will lead our warriors against them!"

"Wait," Powhatan told them. "First we must watch them. Perhaps they do not intend to stay. Let us wait and see."

Powhatan sent Kocoum and Namontack to watch the strange men. They saw the men leave their ship and come onto the land. One man, who seemed to be their leader, planted a flag into the soil. The man spoke strange words in a language Kocoum and Namontack did not understand.

The language was English. The strange men were from England. They came to America to find gold.

"I, Governor Ratcliffe, hereby claim this land for King James of England!" the leader cried. "Have no doubt, men, there is gold in America. Plenty of gold!"

Ashley: It's hard to imagine talking to a tree the way Pocahontas talks to Grandmother Willow.

Mary-Kate: Oh, I don't know. I talk to the dog.

Ashley: Yes, but you don't expect her to answer . . . do you?

Governor Ratcliffe and his men came from England, where Ratcliffe was already a rich and powerful man. But he hoped to find more power and more riches in America.

"If any Indian tries to keep me from that gold, I'll shoot him!" a sailor named Thomas declared.

"Calm down, Thomas!" A tall, blond-haired man grinned. "You are young, and sometimes act before thinking."

"Aye, Captain Smith," Thomas answered, with a nod of respect.

Captain John Smith was always careful to do the right thing. "Leave the Indians to me," John told Thomas. "You just worry about the gold."

Governor Ratcliffe turned to John. "Smith, why don't you explore farther in these woods? See if you find any natives. You other men, grab shovels—and start digging for gold!"

Kocoum and Namontack were startled to see the men chopping down tall, healthy trees. Then the men began digging into the good soil with strange tools. "What are they doing?" Kocoum leaped from behind a tree.

The governor spotted him and Namontack. "Savages!" he shouted. The governor aimed his musket and fired. Namontack was hit in the leg. Kocoum leaped to his friend's side. He hoisted Namontack in his arms and carried him back to the village.

"They invade our shore!" Powhatan cried in anger. "They destroy our land—and they injure my warriors with strange weapons! No one is to go near these white men," he ordered. "Kekata was right. These men are savages!"

Deep in the woods, John Smith knew nothing of the attack on Kocoum and Namontack. He was resting by a waterfall when Pocahontas appeared before him. John gazed at the beautiful girl.

Pocahontas stared back. She had never before seen a man with such white skin, yellow hair, and eyes of blue!

"My name is John Smith," John said clearly.

At first the words were strange to Pocahontas. But she remembered what Grandmother Willow had said: listen with your heart. So she closed her eyes and listened. John repeated the words, and this time, Pocahontas understood.

"My name is Pocahontas," she replied.

Pocahontas and John Smith spoke quietly together, learning about each other.

"My people will build a town here," John told her. "There is so much we can teach you. We have helped savages like you all over the world."

"We are not savages!" Pocahontas cried in anger. John was startled.

"Your people do not know the earth," Pocahontas explained. "They do not treat her as

a living thing, as my people do."

She gazed into John's blue eyes and he felt a sense of deep understanding come over him. "If my men could hear your words, they would forget all about digging for gold."

"Gold?" asked Pocahontas. "What is gold?"

John tried to explain. "It's bright and yellow and comes out of the ground."

"Oh," said Pocahontas. She reached into her bag and pulled out an ear of corn.

"No, that isn't gold." John laughed. He took a gold coin from his pocket and showed it to Pocahontas.

"I have never seen anything like that around here," Pocahontas told him. "But I will ask my father if he has seen this gold."

"Will you meet me tonight?" John asked. He could not bear to let her go.

"Yes," Pocahontas promised. She hurried back to her village, where she found the chief and his braves preparing for war with the white strangers.

"Father," she pleaded. "Try talking with the white men first. They are not all bad!"

"It is not that simple, my daughter," Powhatan replied. "We cannot let these men harm our land."

When John reached his settlement he also found Governor Ratcliffe preparing for battle. The governor showed John a map. "There is gold here!" he declared. "But the Indians are hiding it from us. We will take it from them by force!"

"There *is* no gold!" John declared. "But there is food."

"The Indians don't want to feed us," the governor replied. "They want to kill us! This is *my* land now," he said. "I make the laws here. The law is this: anyone who sees an Indian must kill him!" He glared at John. "Anyone who doesn't will be hanged."

That night, Pocahontas and John Smith sneaked out to meet. They did not know it, but they were both followed. Kocoum followed Pocahontas, and Thomas followed John.

As soon as Pocahontas saw John, she ran to him. "Our warriors are planning to attack your people," she cried.

"My men are planning to attack your village," John replied.

"Please come talk to my father," said Pocahontas. "He will listen to you."

John agreed to speak with Powhatan. Full of joy, Pocahontas kissed him. When Kocoum saw the kiss, he was filled with fury. With a terrible war cry, he burst from his hiding place.

Young Thomas remembered the governor's new law. He aimed his musket and fired. Kocoum fell dead.

Pocahontas cried out in pain and disbelief. "You killed Kocoum!" she sobbed.

"Thomas, get out of here," John ordered. "Now!"

Moments later, the glade was filled with Powhatan's warriors. They seized John and dragged him back to their village. Pocahontas followed, feeling helpless. She loved her people—but now she loved John, too.

Chief Powhatan was saddened by Kocoum's death. And he was furious with Pocahontas.

"Kocoum is dead because you disobeyed me and left the village," Powhatan told her. He pointed to John Smith. "Take the prisoner away!"

That night, Pocahontas crept into the tent where John was kept prisoner. "I cannot bear to leave you," she told him.

"No matter what happens, I will be with you—forever," John told her.

Pocahontas raced to her canoe. She paddled downriver to ask Grandmother Willow for advice.

"Grandmother, tell me what to do! I must save John Smith," she said.

"Listen with your heart," Grandmother Willow instructed.

Pocahontas was still. She waited for wisdom to fill her heart. "Thank you, Grandmother," she whispered. She jumped back into her canoe and headed home.

Pocahontas arrived as the new day was breaking. Her father stood over John Smith, his war club raised high. At that moment, Governor Ratcliffe and his men burst out of the trees with their muskets raised, ready to fire.

"No!" Pocahontas threw herself across John to protect him. Surprised, Ratcliffe's soldiers stopped still.

Pocahontas raised her eyes to her father's face. "If you kill John, you will have to kill me, too," Pocahontas exclaimed. "Please, Father, look around you. Everyone is full of anger and hatred. I choose not to hate. That is my special path. What will your path be?"

Powhatan gazed at his brave daughter. His face softened.

"My daughter speaks wisely," he said. "Release the prisoner!"

Governor Ratcliffe stared at Powhatan in surprise. Suspicion and fear still filled his heart. "Now is our chance, men! Fire your muskets!" he ordered.

Thomas glanced at Pocahontas. Then he lowered his musket. "I will not fire a shot," he declared. "I also choose not to hate."

One by one, the other men lowered their muskets.

"I'll do it myself, then!" Governor Ratcliffe seized a musket and fired at Chief Powhatan.

John Smith pushed Powhatan out of the way. The chief was saved. But John was struck. He fell to the ground.

"John is injured!" Thomas cried. "Put the governor in chains!"

Now the governor was a prisoner, and the Englishmen did not have to follow his orders anymore. They tore down their fort. Some of them prepared to sail back to England, tak-

ing John with them. He would need a doctor's care if he was to live.

"I don't want to leave you," John told Pocahontas.

"You never will," Pocahontas replied. "No matter what happens, I will be with you. Forever."

With a full heart, Pocahontas waved good-bye. She and John Smith would each follow a different path. But she knew that he would tell her story to all of England—the story of a brave Indian maiden who had shown it was better to chose peace over war, and to choose love over hatred and fear. It was a story that deserves to be told again and again, as we have told it now.

Pocahontas's Dream-Come-True Dream Catcher

Mary-Kate and I both think dream catchers are really special. They're supposed to catch your bad dreams, so you keep only the good ones! We hung our dream catchers in our favorite bedroom window. Choose a special place to catch your dreams, too!

You'll Need

- Plates in three different sizes to trace (we used 6", 8", 12")

- Markers

- A piece of oaktag or other heavy paper

- Two pieces of felt; choose two different colors, as large as your largest plate

- Scissors

- A hole punch

- Yarn; about three yards

- Beads

- Glue

- Feathers

How to Make It

1. Take the largest plate and with your marker, trace a circle onto the oaktag. Cut out the circle.

2. Trace another circle the same size onto one color of felt. Cut out the circle.

3. Take the medium-sized plate and with your marker, trace a circle onto the second color of felt. Cut out the circle.

4. Take the small-sized plate and with your marker, trace a circle centered in the middle of the large-sized oaktag circle, the large-sized felt circle, and the medium-sized felt circle.

5. Cut out the center circles. You should have three circles with holes in the middle—like a doughnut. (See picture.)

6. Punch two holes in the oaktag circle, about 1 inch apart, near the outer edge—this will be the top of your dream catcher.

7. Punch six holes in the oaktag circle, about 1 inch apart, along the outside edge of the circle opposite the two holes. (See picture.)

8. Take the oaktag circle and punch a row of holes 1 inch apart around the entire *center* hole of the circle.

9. Cut a 6-inch length of yarn. Insert the ends through the top holes of the oaktag then tie to make a hanger.

10. Cut six pieces of yarn into 12-inch lengths. Tie one end of each piece around each of the six bottom holes of the oaktag circle. String a few beads onto each piece of yarn. Knot each bead in place. Glue a feather to the end of each piece.

11. Thread the remaining piece of yarn in and out of the holes lining the center hole of the oaktag circle. Make an interesting pattern. (See the picture for an example.) While threading the yarn, you can add more beads for decoration.

12. When the yarn is threaded through all the holes, cut the end and glue to the back of the oaktag.

13. Glue the two pieces of felt together, so the smaller piece is centered on top of the larger piece. Glue feathers onto the felt for trim.

14. Glue the felt circles to the oaktag.

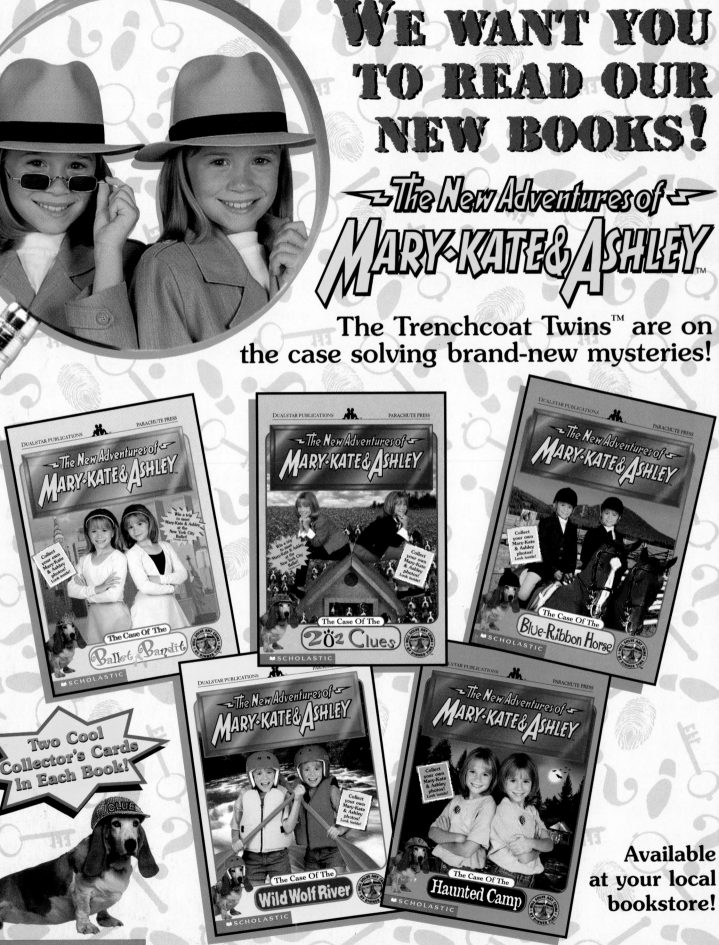

Pick Up All-New Party Fun

from **MARY-KATE & ASHLEY**

YOU'RE INVITED TO MARY-KATE & ASHLEY'S **Ballet Party**
Based on NEW YORK CITY BALLET
A MUSICAL PARTY SERIES
DUALSTAR VIDEO

YOU'RE INVITED TO MARY-KATE & ASHLEY'S **CAMP OUT PARTY**
A MUSICAL PARTY SERIES
DUALSTAR VIDEO

Win
a trip to
New York City,
see New York City Ballet and
meet Mary-Kate & Ashley
or win Coleman Kids camping gear.

DUALSTAR VIDEO

Listen To Us!

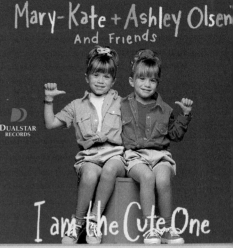

© & TM 1998 Dualstar Entertainment Group, Inc.